Furious in the Expanse

Fierce fires by
Yarrow Paisley

Furious in the Expanse
by Yarrow Paisley
ISBN: 978-1-913766-01-6

Cover Art by David Rix

Publication Date: November 2021

These pieces appeared—variously altered—in *Web Conjunctions*, *Ragshock Four*, *Sein und Werden*, *Cavalier Literary Couture*, *Gone Lawn*, and the *Step Chamber*.

Table of Contents

Down the heavy sunk; cleaving around
To the fragments of solid: up rose
The thin, flowing round the fierce fires
That glow'd furious in the expanse.

The Book of Los, III:6., W Blake, 1795.

Preface

An Autobiographical Note

As far as I could tell, there was no excessive jubilation on my return to my provenance. Fanfares played, true, and streamers shot up, but these well could have been in response to some coincidental event. I am not one to presume.

Listing on a street corner was my father, holding a sign and gazing out of dazed eyes at passersby. The sign was not written in the language of the people who passed, and he received no donations. He did not appear to notice this negligence, the daze of his eyes being steady and committed; but he held the sign fiercely.

I spoke briefly to him, demanding no response, merely practicing the performance of my speech. My words took on the forms of his hallucinations, and he smiled vaguely, replying in this way despite my assertion of no need. His voice began to hum. I appreciated the effort and left him there to his pursuits.

I did not seek certainty after that, and did not mind its lack.

The world became a ruin from my inattention. How passionately I sat upon the crumbling benches beneath those monuments! How ardently I gazed upon the mounds! All my capacity for love swelled into a bubble in my mouth, which I batted gently with my tongue until my pent breath burst through the seam of my lips and released the bubble into the world, never to be seen again.

How can the biography be written of a man who can't remember? Ask his consorts, I suppose. They shall remember every failure, and they will not suppress one detail of his impotence, in the interest of historical veracity. And what better way to ensure sales?

I retain glimmerings of that time, however. Nothing can be entirely erased. There is always some smudge left on the surface. The smudge bears all the burdens of meanings it no longer signifies. It does not resent the meanings, just the burdens. They weigh much, contribute nothing.

I cannot relate the consciousness of the smudge, but all my yearning will carry it toward you. You shall be responsible only to stand in one spot so I can find you even with my eyes downcast and my ears filled with the scream of ululations that may or may not be the exertion of my own lungpower.

Things may have happened one way or another; there is not much difference as far as I can tell. As an object passes by another, gravitation becomes felt in degrees that match proximity. This is natural, and shall circumvention be attempted, it shall be thwarted. And will you move your lips as you read this piece? I am not watching; no one is. But there is no shame in it.

I sought an absolute record of events, an account of history without omission, infinite in scope and minuscule in reading time. I am impatient of reading materials. I wish to finish once I've started, and once I've finished I wish I'd savored, but it is too late; and afterward, one merely sits and stares.

I craved treats without consequence, and never could find them. Always sold out. On order. I placed my name on waiting lists. The outlets would close before my name was reached, their proprietors satisfied with the profits-to-date and admirably not greedy for more.

My cravings intensified. I manufactured simulacra of those objects I desired. They are with me now, in the form of dust, into which they have disintegrated. I have not bothered to reconstitute them. They would only return to dust again.

How far must one travel, I asked myself. If home is farther from you than that world you most despise, is it a matter of strength to surpass the near to reach the far, or endurance? Shall you summon energy or will? Or shall you merely shut your eyes and wait? And do you have the choice?

I believed for some time that I had fooled myself. The place I had come to bore superficial resemblance to that which I sought, but surely these faces were shifted somewhat out of the sublime molds of my memory. Certainly, there was upon them the crust of a suffering which had no existence in my recollections:

The man with his eyes fixed to a plate of clear glass as though it were a mirror of himself—this man could not be the one who'd laughed as a boy at the onslaughts of history and called them winds more fetid than the breathing of butts! And he prying ineffectually at the fastened lid of his own snuffbox, this one could not be the scholar of exotic percussions whose rhythms transcended in complexity even the mating trills of birds.

Perfection lurked in the corners of every room I entered, but no broom could sweep it out into clear light. Wedged in its preferred nooks, it remained ungraspable.

I celebrated what I could not achieve, however, by simulating it in substandard forms and imprinting on it publicly the brand of my satisfaction. I deferred my weeping to private moments.

A city descended around me. Buildings fell into place. Wherever I lingered, new structures floated down upon readymade foundations. I did not doubt my surroundings. There is no doubt without questions, and I could summon none.

Instead, my imagination latched onto the provisions of my survival. About me were the records of human endeavor, and I persuaded myself of their authenticity.

I sought the shadows of my visions. Such light, however, as was cast upon them passed through undeflected.

One must hold the world in his mind, I came to understand. All that becomes and fades shall not be lost. The qualities of objects are themselves objects; transparency and opaqueness stand separately as viewable entities. The eye which grasps an object holds it should even demolition attempt to break the grip. Memory preserves the existence of all things. Even the faulty and diffident objects of the world shall persevere alongside the perfect and mighty. There shall come a time in which no distinctions can be drawn.

However may one console himself with perceptions of intersections of time and existence, one must eat.

There were no fruit sellers on my block. Only dung could be had, and dearly. One must die, who lives on dung: had not my mother taught me this? Had not his mother, the seller's? How had he come upon this form of commerce? Stumbled into it, or craftily designed it from the bottom up? I did not ask the man, nor did I ask his competitor. I bowed my head in greeting and exchanged a friendly word, even as I hated him. I hated him so hotly that I felt my burning should ignite the nugget

I held. And yet, at the transaction's conclusion we receded from each other, and these passions dwindled, on my side at least.

Everywhere, revenants touched the world, and my own body trembled as though all should crumble at such contact. But all things remained fixed in their bodies, as did I remain fixed in mine.

My expectations laid me low. I wept at the sight of a cat sliding along brick.

I wept when the rain did not pass through me but entered me through the pores.

I wept when my weeping came to sustain me in the nights when I felt I should dissolve into my cushions.

At the door of history, I paused. The lintel was carved of ivory, the sill was ice. Between the two, jambs of mirror.

I dared not step through. I feared my feet.

And yet, on the other side was a room whose walls were lined with shelves upon which were stored books of all materials and sizes. They beckoned me, as books do.

Still, I dared not step through. I feared I would be forbidden to remove any of those books, no matter how mysterious and compelling the words they contained. I feared I would be trapped in that room with those books, bound to them as surely as their pages were bound to their bindings.

And yet, what kept me here but provenance? With what chains did my provenance secure me to the world of ghosts and bodies?

I could not answer, but the chains, as solid as the mind they harnessed, tugged me back from all doors out of the world.

We Must Have Faith

You must be breathless in our time. The decree is modern, the populace yet unaccustomed to its firm mandate. We cannot quite comprehend the necessity of breathlessness; not yet. Indeed, it would seem antithetical: *breath* should be the order of the day: this is the common feeling, albeit a covert one as it would not be wise to advertise a deficiency of faith in law.

I am of the faithful, I assure you. There is no lack in *me* as regards my citizenship. I hold fervent trust within my heart: trust in law: trust in innocence: trust in our poet-king. I hold trust within my heart because not to would mean an end to my heart—eviction from society and sanity. I mean to be social. I mean to be sane. I mean to keep a healthy heart. Nothing will deter me from my goals.

I have been practicing breathlessness every day since the decree was published. It has been almost nine years now. It is a question of will. Who but our brilliant poet-king could have understood that the praxis of will is the *true axis* of human soul? that the action of will being the soul duty of man, must be the sole duty of a man? that man's greatness lies in the immortality of his soul? that immortality being a function of soul may be achieved *on earth* therefore only through the transubstantiation of body into soul? that will is the only possible engine of this miracle?

Everything that breathes, dies. A nation must end whose citizens breathe.

I saw our poet-king once on parade, a year before the decree. He waved to the crowds. He was weeping, I could not tell from joy or sorrow. Some feeling rose in me, a hammer knocked within my beating heart. I shouted with the mob, I could not tell from joy or sorrow. I shouted till my lungs burned, and I was weeping too, weeping with my king.

I wept with our king.

My wife lacks in faith. She means well, I assure you, hers is a *good heart*. I love her.

But she questions the law. Now: here: she says: "Arthur, breath is good. *Must* life be everlasting? Perhaps a breath every now and then would do us good."

I cannot abide: I explain it to her as patiently as I can: but I confess sometimes my passion conquers me: I shout: I violate the very decree I am so zealously defending: my wife folds her arms and beams: I take her here and now: I shout the name of our poet-king throughout my throes: my wife shrieks her pleasure: I am done: like a dog

I slink to my room, shame-faced, vowing eternal breathlessness. *Love does not require breath*, I shout from my room. I hear my wife's laughter.

It is a question of will. We must have faith.

Everything that breathes, dies. *A nation must end whose citizens breathe.*

Ten is Enough

I live in ten towns, and keep ten families. None know of the others. I did not think it meet to introduce them. They are happy thinking they are each alone.

I know all my children's names by heart. There are fifty-two children. Many mouths to feed, as the saying goes. Fortunately, I am exceedingly rich, and feeding all those mouths has proven no difficulty at all.

My business requires extensive traveling, and so my wives are duped as to the true reason for my frequent absences. They keep house and raise my children, and during the brief interludes of my presence, their faces light up with smiles and laughter. Every one of them loves me dearly. I provide for them and the children, I am a virile lover when home, a scrupulous correspondent when "abroad," I take them on vacations every two years (every two months for me), I encourage them to pursue their individual interests and hobbies with the aid of a sizable allowance from my own purse: what more could they desire in a man?

I used to have eleven families, but one of my wives found out about the others: a letter I left carelessly out on my desk. She threatened a divorce and hinted she would find all my wives and inform them of my polygamy. I pleaded and cajoled to the best of my persuasion, but to no avail. Sadly, in order to preserve the peace and sanctity of my other families, I was forced to kill her and the children as well.

I have not sought a replacement. Ten families is enough for one man, I think.

Cherry Soda

There is a path, secret, behind my house. Although it is not on my land, it can be seen and accessed only from my property. I do not know where it leads. I have never been down it.

Over the years, I have been curious about that path. It is a long-ingrained habit of mine to sit in my rocker on the back porch, drinking cherry soda, gazing down the path as far as I can see. The path is lined with strange yellow grasses. They do not grow anywhere else in this area, to the best of my knowledge. The grasses are stiff, bend only before the strongest of gales. I have seen a wind sweep down that path that rose the dirt in angry whorls—the grasses in their posture perdured, effortless. Yes, they are insouciant grasses.

Once, about a year ago, the three of us—my wife, my son, and myself—awoke to the sound of a shrill shrieking laughter. We stood in the backyard and listened for hours. It continued till dawn, then stopped. I sent my son down the path to investigate. He has not yet returned. I have not given up hope. It has only been a year. I tell my wife, "Give him time. He's a slow-witted boy, but eventually he gets the idea." My wife is not convinced, but I do not concern myself with her grumblings. She grumbles—it is an attribute of hers that I have learned over the course of our marriage to filter out. She grumbles even as she brings me my cherry soda.

When my son returns, I will have many questions to ask him. But there is one in particular I am most keen to ask: "What is so funny that grasses must laugh?"

Death & Harleys

On the occasion of my daughter's death, I was not present. She was struck by a truck. (The rhyme is quite unintentional.) The truck carried fuel. My daughter was not killed by the impact of the vehicle, but by the explosion which ensued when the driver in his confusion caused the truck to topple and spill its contents, which were ignited by the sparks of its endless skid. My daughter was burned beyond recognition. The funeral was a closed-casket affair. Fortunately, my wife had died already (Harley mishap at a drive-thru window) and was not subject to the grief which I was forced to endure, being alive.

I had nightmares for a year. In one dream, my daughter came to me and pulled my blankets from off my nude form. I found I was tied and gagged, helpless to her lascivious designs. She bathed my body in her pubescent fluids, and my involuntary ecstasy horrified and sickened me. She grinned without a trace of her former pep. She seemed a corpse, but for the flush of her desire.

In another dream, my wife rode in on her Harley, which was ornamented with my daughter's limbs and head. My wife dismounted, strode vulgarly, slapped her leather-clad thighs and set them jiggling. Her breasts grew out of her blouse and smothered me.

In another dream, I held my daughter above my head. She screamed, but her voice was lost in the storm which gathered, the rain, the wind. I held her above my head and waded through a flood, but I slipped and went under. When I came up, I could not see her. I began to float down a river, my face serene under a starry sky.

After the nightmares subsided, I met a woman. She resembled my daughter strikingly. We married. I sired children on her. She came home with a Harley one day, fresh from the dealership: I beat her, told her to take it back, I would permit no Harleys in my home. She rode off, and never returned—she was struck by a truck.

I am raising the children myself. I do not let them out of my sight. They are mine. They will not die.

An Instinct for Beauty

When I was a child, I murdered my sister. I did not do this because I hated her, or was abused by an adult, or unduly influenced by rock and roll: I did it out of an instinct for beauty.

You see, I loved nothing else in the world but my sister. We spent all our time together: playing in the backyard, telling each other stories, forever giggling and tickling. Laughter predominated in our relationship. Smiles and caresses.

One day I experienced a waking dream: my sister's body, crushed and bloody. The dream lasted for one hour: I hovered five feet above her and observed her silence, her stasis, her eternal beauty.

I loved her so much that I knew I must consummate my vision of her perfect death. Had time passed, had she grown old with me, the character of our love most certainly would have altered; for our love was innocent, and with age our innocence would have diminished. Any number of factors might have contributed to this metamorphosis: life experience, ambition, the introduction of other people into our lives: but the most crucial factor—and the prevailing one in my decision to end her life—was the inevitable development of the body through adolescence into adulthood. As a woman, she would be my sister, but not the sister I loved and cherished *at that moment*. Even as a child, I understood this, and knew that the only way to immortalize my sister, and our love, was to curtail immediately this development.

To this day, I carry with me the image of her body, crushed and bloody. The image is silent, static, eternal. The passage of time has not altered her beauty one bit. Her innocence remains with me, and I am innocent.

Rapture in Stillness

Absolutely still. The subject may not move, that is my unwavering policy. If she moves, I fire her. She is cast out into the merciless world. They rarely make the mistake, they are quite conscious of the dangers. Death is inevitable out there. In here, there is safety. She may eat, she may sleep, she may relax in the knowledge that her sexual innocence is and will remain intact.

Absolutely still. The subject earns her keep. I eat my dinner, gazing, insulated in my world of beauty. All around me, wealth glitters. And before me, she is still. Her eyes are mannequin eyes. Her brow is the imperturbable brow of an ancient goddess. Her lips are stone lips. She is clad in gowns, brocades, lace. She is ornamented in pearls, diamonds, metals of the finest sheen. A body draped in wealth, and it is mine: body and wealth. I could gaze all night. I am so rich, I need not even wank myself, but have hired special servants to perform that task. I may be as still as she, and yet still surge in ecstasy. While she is stone, I am flesh, and her strength is my weakness.

Absolutely still. Sometimes I cannot prevent myself: I approach. I gaze from on close. I gaze up. Up into the deep of her beauty, her wealth. Up into the deep of her stony stillness. Beneath the stone, a heart beats. The stone is not stone, but is flesh, but through my will alone, through my wealth, the flesh is made stone. I have this power, I am giddy with it. In my mind, I shriek into her stillness, and her stillness perdures. In my mind, I claw at her breasts, I tear her wealth from her body: she is naked flesh: she is stone: I press myself against her: she is stone: I claw at her breasts, draw the blood out, bequeath pain unto her as would charge flesh *scream*: she is stone: she is still. In my moments of perfection, I am, in her company, alone.

Absolutely still. My mind achieves this wonder in the after-time: I lie in my bed, draped in wealth, draped in darkness, draped in imaginings of my living statue. I know she is standing in the darkness beside me, absolutely still, although I cannot see her. I have hired her to be still, and she earns her keep.

The Cat of Unknowing

There is something hideous in the features of my face. I cannot isolate this factor, not entirely, but it casts a decidedly diabolical scheme into my expressions, which is not there by intention, but by nature. I appear at all times to be things I am not.

Midgets have accosted me on the street with great joviality and slaps on the back, claiming me of their kind, although I am quite tall. Children have persecuted me for my irregular nose, although it is classically straight. Women have attempted to seduce me, believing me virile, a veritable movie star, although I am impotent and have been since grade school. Talent scouts have pinched my arms and cheeks, awed at my muscle tone and general charismatic fiber, although I am an on the whole unremarkable physical specimen. Drunks have staggered home on my arm, believing me their sober buddy, when in truth my staggering exceeded theirs.

A cat leapt out of a tree the other day, landing on my head. It stayed there for several hours, a comfortable cat. I quite enjoyed its warmth and weight. I was struck with a sense of loss and emptiness when the cat dismounted with a view to a bird on the neighbor's lawn. I watched that cat pounce, I watched the bird's blood burble out, I watched the cat lick its paws. The cat looked back at me for a moment. I felt it saw me, saw my face true: in its bored eyes was a recognition of the hideous factor in my features, the one I could never isolate. I leapt to my feet, prepared to beseech of the cat an answer to my eternal question: "Why am I the opposite of all I ever am?" But the cat looked away, disinterested. I pleaded for my answer: the cat purred. I killed the cat in frustration, and held its body in my arms for a while until I realized it could not have answered me: cats do not speak.

I will inter the cat soon in a proper burial plot. But first I will buy a mirror, and place the cat behind it. I will look into the mirror—I'll never cease but when I see the cat.

A Siege Mentality

This city has been under siege for too long. And I have been under the city's siege. The blocks have every day encroached upon the borders of my mind: the vacant buildings, the crumbling walls, the screech of children's throats between the zinging bullets, the laughter of the soldiers on the open street passing cigarette-mouthed as I crouch in my huddling-corners, the sexual moaning of the earth under penetration of mines and mortars, the sky's smoky breath in the midnights and noons of everlasting suns and moons. I have been under siege, and my family weeps my tears since my own tears have gone in aid of our city's defense. The fathers assured us the siege would not last long, but they were wrong, I do not blame them, how could they know, but I blame them, how could they assure us, those feeble men, how could they?

I am under the city's siege. Portions of my mind every day by justification of eminent domain are annexed to those streets. My mind grows smaller, the streets encroach.

My youngest child in rags tugs at my rags, and my hand flies to meet her cheek, the brat flies to meet her mother, child cries, mother cries, I do not cry. The public works have taken my tears, in order to supply all available moisture to the parched throats of our valiant soldiers. The streets encroach, my mind grows smaller.

In my mind, angels are above the city, smiling in flight, floating in laughter, golden gowns sweeping peace beneath those folds.

In my mind, the city is small.

In my mind, love keeps my family with me, and love keeps me with my family.

In my mind, horror flees. In my mind, there is a soothing salty tide come washing through these streets. In my mind, the fathers have ordained we all must live, and never die. In my mind, the battalions have thrown down their guns—immersed themselves in great orgies in the streets—a soothing salty tide of sex has come washing through these streets—I have cleaned my face in that soothing salty tide—I have bathed my family's flesh in that soothing salty tide.

In my mind, there is celebration for the city's liberation.

But the city has been under siege for too long, and I am under the city's siege—the streets encroach, my mind grows smaller.

A House in the Hills

There is a house in the hills to which I sometimes take myself. It is not my house, I do not know who owns it. I take myself there and lay myself in the hammock which hangs perpetually in its backyard. I swing back and forth with my hands clasped for pillow, elbows jutting at right angles for balance. Above me, above the leafy branches above me, above the airplanes skimming overhead those branches, there is space for my eyes to travel whilst my body swings.

My right eye prefers to fly among the planets. It disguises itself: becomes an orb of nova diamond forged in the time before the planets. The planets regard my eye as some kind of emissary from the ancient solar god they fear, and sweep respectfully out of its path when they detect its approach. The diamond eye makes its rounds. It once fell in love with a Jupiter moon, but the moon hewed close to her father out of bashfulness born of terror, *but too close*, and she fell into her father's sea. My diamond eye flew onward.

My left eye loves to spread. As it flies high, its density decreases. By the time it reaches the solar system's circumference, it *is* the solar system's circumference. By the time it reaches the galactic rim, my left eye contains the whole galaxy. The galaxy never notices, nor does the solar system. But my left eye is content to be invisible. Were it visible, no celestial mass would suffer it to so expand: it would be crushed by these jealous bodies: interstellar pulp floating forevermore homeless.

When my arms grow tired, my eyes return. I break into the house and prepare some food. I do not feel guilty, for the owners of the house are rich and can easily afford my occasional forays into their pantry. It is my impression, in fact, that they've never even noticed.

Humid Thesis

And so, with that humid atmosphere incessantly channeled into my room, I grew giddy. The moisture seeped deep in my hot lungs; my breath was water, and my brain was steam. I lived more perfectly in tune with the structure of my constituents. I learned of purity, and balance: the soul is waterless, and so must be the body waterlogged. That everlasting dose of water in my breath served me well. I imagined a future society in which every boy's and girl's room would be equipped with devices for channeling in some humid sort of atmosphere. I vowed to make my dream manifest if I must devote my entire lifespan to its advocacy. At first, the general public was suspicious of my unorthodox ideas, but when the results came in, those suspicions slackened. Trust rose, stocks soared. Soon I was among the world's richest men. Every room in the nation was outfitted with my special patented device. Every nose inhaled of that needed moisture. I never ceased in my giddiness. I am yet giddy. I will continue to be giddy for as long as I shall live.

The Thirty Days of Bellesgrant & Zerxaquarius

In fury—haggard—flailing—weary. Thus were his energies depleted. There was confusion of a bipolar nature. He could not choose an extreme, and both claimed him. They divided him up between each other. They cooed, he gibbered. They named him: one Bellesgrant, the other Zerxaquarius. Naturally, he did not know which to prefer. At times he was Bellesgrant, at times Zerxaquarius. More and more, he came to be both simultaneously; he accomplished this by splitting into two distinct identities, by no means mutually exclusive, but independent and unique of each other nonetheless.

There were great wars in the ancient times. Bellesgrant fought them. He examined their qualities, and reproduced them in his mind, and rebuilded them anew: modern, lethal. Bellesgrant was history's tactician. His insight into the martial philosophies was so keen and artful that had he been both generals in the first war, there would only ever have been fought *one war*, and that war would still now be raging in stalemate. His every defense perfectly checked his every offensive, and his every counteroffensive was perfectly checked by his every reciprocal defense.

Zerxaquarius filled out forms. There were blank spaces on these forms, crying for calligraphic opacity. He made every underlined space *mean something*. He gave each its due, and its proper respect. He deliberated all the potential inksweepings through those spaces (positioned carefully atop those lines), their form suggested by neatly printed subline (or sometimes supra-) instructions. Through a complex process, he calibrated the journey of his pen, the exact yet meandering route, the country through which that nib would trek. He negotiated with native bearers, calculated distance so not to overshoot the objective, maintained the integrity of his ink supply (for ink was his medium, and no other would suffice).

This was what Bellesgrant carved in that tree: *I am immortal.* When the tree was chopped and converted to lumber, Bellesgrant traced the distribution of its boards and planks. Each building, and every furniture piece, and all the objects fashioned from that tree: *Bellesgrant burned them.* He inhaled the smoke of all the blazes. His lungs turned black, and shriveled.

One day in the garden, Zerxaquarius sipping his wine imagined that a fine day was: *precisely one such as he was experiencing:* yet the day did not to him feel so fine. He pondered this for a while sipping his wine until the wine was finished. Then he went to sleep and dreamed of Bellesgrant.

Bellesgrant waited in the shadows. Finally, a petite woman walked by, and Bellesgrant leaped out, took her struggling limbs in his arms, closed her in his body, entered back into the shadows. There he subdued her. He pierced her bright eyes with the twin brass wires he kept coiled in his belt.

He sought the secret of her brain. She did not relinquish it. He wondered what Zerxaquarius was doing right now. This woman's brain was frustrating him. He devoured it, and when he was sated he played with her breasts.

There is something perverse in the way that man watches me, thought Zerxaquarius. The man in question had been watching Zerxaquarius for over an hour, without blinking or nodding or changing the position of his buttocks against the hard chair surface. That chair is constructed of steel and cold iron, thought Zerxaquarius. His muscles must be in agony by now (as mine are). But the man still did not move. Zerxaquarius watched him for a long time.

In the witching hour, Bellesgrant carried a heavy sack. It undulated languidly, bulging and flattening in unexpected places. Bellesgrant utilized his own sharp fingers to dig a hole deep in the soft loam. He tossed the sack, which was by now writhing, into the hole. Quickly, Bellesgrant refilled the hole, then made away into the woods as dawn approached.

Occasionally Zerxaquarius induced a promising girl to fall in love with him. He utilized her for purposes of masturbation, for he found it much pleasanter to stimulate himself in the orifice of a young girl than in the orifice of his own hand. When he broke the girl's heart (as well as her hymen), he was careful to effect a lasting and utterly permanent damage, so as to be certain that she never would be happy with another man. This increased his pleasure in the sexual act. He felt he had one up on Bellesgrant.

There was a place Bellesgrant went to when he needed of rest. It was a place of bones and cobwebs, mildewed, mossy, rank. The bed there was soft, however, and the blanket provided a surprising share of warmth considering how patched and thin was its material. Yet Bellesgrant slept fitfully. He was comfortable, and this made him uneasy.

Once Zerxaquarius stubbed his toe and wept for three hours as a consequence. He vowed never to stub his toe again, but it happened again, and this time he wept for four hours. He did not know what to do, for it seemed quite possible that he would stub his toe a third time, and what if he never stopped weeping? Thus, he borrowed an axe from his neighbor (an executioner by trade) and with it removed his toe. Bellesgrant would approve of my solution, he thought. He returned the axe promptly.

The liquids surged into frangible forms. The metals fucked the light prismatic. He rose up through the trees to look out over the landscape, but saw only the white beauty of the villas. His body varied in density as an oscillating function of time. He wept, and this was painful, for his tears were crystal.

Zerxaquarius hired a servant to clean after him. The servant, of indeterminate gender, face pallid and immobile, followed Zerxaquarius throughout the mansion, mute, somber, in its hand a dustpan and a rag. Zerxaquarius grew so accustomed to the servant's presence that he forgot he had hired a servant. One day Zerxaquarius thought, I ought to hire a servant to clean after me. That very day he did so. When the servant, of indeterminate gender, arrived, it joined a troupe which followed Zerxaquarius, making the number thirteen. The others, superstitious of the number, killed it that night while it slept. They were efficient in their disposal of the body, since cleaning was their *métier*.

On a road, Bellesgrant encountered a boy with broken legs. The boy breathed only faintly, too weak even to raise its head, yet it regarded Bellesgrant with insolent eyes. Bellesgrant took sticks and tied the boy's legs into splints. The boy found a voice to say, *Thank you*. Bellesgrant did not reply, but continued on his way.

Zerxaquarius devoured an entire pheasant in one sitting, yet he was still hungry. He went to the icebox, but there were no more pheasants to be had. His craving for pheasant consumed him. He searched the icebox again. He thought, Save me

Bellesgrant. Zerxaquarius pondered the pheasant situation until, that night, he slept. The next morning he resumed his pondering.

Bellesgrant fell through a space which was located in the center of a gorge. There was more space below him as yet than above, but this proportion was steadily reversing itself. Soon he would be at the ground, and the lip of the gorge from which he had leaped would be but a tiny memory, never regained, for he knew that no one may climb the cliff but only leave it, as he had done. It occurred to him that Zerxaquarius might be *up there*, but it was too late to meet him. Perhaps Zerxaquarius would be *down there*. All the while, he continued to fall.

The poem spoke of beauty. Zerxaquarius remained unmoved. He turned the page. The next poem spoke of eternity. Zerxaquarius remained unmoved, and turned the page. The next poem spoke of seven diamonds in seven corners. It spoke of: the faces in the facets; the cleaving silence; the lethal angle; the eye which migrates through the structure. Zerxaquarius turned the page.

Bellesgrant slogged through the marsh. The waters stank, these weeds rank, these swamps permeated through with the discarded waste of every living process and the putrefied remnants of long dead organisms. The matter soaked his clothes, seeped through his open pores, toxified his fluids. He grew ill, and slogged on. He grew cold, and slogged on. He slowed, but on he slogged. Bellesgrant thought about Zerxaquarius.

There was a rotten board in the house of Zerxaquarius. Occasionally Zerxaquarius thought, I must replace the board. But the board remained in place, for Zerxaquarius always forgot. One day, the board stove in under his weight, and Zerxaquarius fell, dislocating his thumb. After he had shifted the thumb back into its socket Zerxaquarius thought, I will replace the board. Bellesgrant must not know.

In his pocket, Bellesgrant carried a silver locket. The locket was important to him, although he did not recall how he had acquired it and he did not recognize the man and the woman whose pictures adorned the interior frames. The day came when Bellesgrant reached into his pocket to touch the smoothness of the locket only to discover in its place a ragged hole. Maddened, Bellesgrant struck his chest and into his own flesh embedded the locket which he had earlier removed from his pocket and draped around his neck. After this, Bellesgrant's attachment to the locket dwindled. When he really did lose it some time later, he did not even notice.

Zerxaquarius purchased a brand new deck of playing cards. The first time he shuffled them, he thought, Once is not enough, so he shuffled them again. Zerxaquarius regarded the cards, and thought, If once was not enough then why should twice be? So he shuffled them again. Zerxaquarius continued to shuffle the cards well into the dawn of the next day. His heart pounded, his fingers were numb and stiff, his eyes contained denser orbs within them: and he continued to shuffle. He did not stop until he fainted from exhaustion.

Bellesgrant's clothes dissolved in the sandstorm. When the gales abated and the sands settled, Bellesgrant trudged naked through the desert. A scorpion lanced his Achilles tendon. Some parasite invaded his genitals. His eyes crusted shut with a mixture of mucus and sand grains. Eventually he made it to the trading post. He purchased what he needed, for the proprietor accepted his credit. The proprietor mentioned Zerxaquarius, but Bellesgrant made no reply.

He lay on the water and raised his arms. He shut both eyes against the sky brightness. He felt weak, yet something was building in his belly. There was a toothglobed entity revolving in there. He moaned with two voices.

Zerxaquarius lay abed, feverish. He had been thus for a week now. His fever would neither increase nor decrease, but remained exactly as it was. In his brain there was a vision in thirty dimensions, vivid and terrible, accreting detail with every instant that passed. He saw a statue in his garden, one which never had been there before. It was noble, and venerated. It would be remembered, and people would come, passing through the garden, to see it. No one knew whose garden this was, but inscribed in the pedestal which supported the statue was the word *Bellesgrant.*

Bellesgrant hewed down the orchard. His hysteria did not abate. The field next to this one was splendid and beautiful, but there was a fence between the fields. Enraged, Bellesgrant flung himself at this fence, chopped at its posts with the bare blade of his hand. When the fence was razed he felt tired. He noticed that the trees in this new orchard provided shade and lush bedding. He climbed into one and went to sleep in its branches. He never saw the feral girl who came out of hiding when he was finally unconscious and crawled onto his chest to feel him breathe. She bit off the tip of his nose as a souvenir and scampered away, but Bellesgrant did not even wake up.

At the theatre, Zerxaquarius fell in love with the actress. He recalled the blaze of his fever, and preferred that to *this blaze*. He imagined the tortures of the profanest mind, and too preferred them to *this torture*. He waited in the wings, a shadow in the shadows, until he saw the actress alone. From his wings of hiding, Zerxaquarius watched her in her boudoir. He waited all night until she was dead. In the morning he went home and made breakfast.

All the rocks were tumbling around him, but Bellesgrant continued unharmed along his way. Once a stone the size of a pheasant's egg struck him in the back of the head. He touched his fingers periodically to the lump which there developed, but he continued along his way. After a few hours he became woozy and disoriented. There were no rocks anymore, so he lay down in the grass and went to sleep, even though the sun was still high in the sky. He slept for thirty hours.

Zerxaquarius knelt at the window which overlooked his garden. He had not moved from this position all day, not since he had noticed a movement *down there* this morning. He did not dare to move away from the window for fear that the moment he did so the movement *down there* would resume. I *will* see it, he thought.

Bellesgrant came to the city, having heard the stories. The bustle of the crowds baffled him, though, and as the day wore on he found himself more confused and more flustered than he had ever been. No one stopped to gaze on Bellesgrant. He was carried along on the street tide, only flotsam in a tremendous ocean. The faces he glimpsed (the crests of the waves) were impassive and absorbed: pallid, immobile. But one face in the crowd terrified him, so that he left the city immediately.

Feeling not himself, Zerxaquarius paced restlessly through his mansion. He came to the conclusion that he should join a mountain-climbing expedition. He signed on to one immediately. The expedition was preempted halfway up the mountainside when a flaw in the rope claimed three lives. Enraged, Zerxaquarius demanded a refund. Zerxaquarius returned to his mansion feeling not himself, and he paced restlessly through the corridors. (He noticed that every room was very clean.)

Bellesgrant moaned and shivered in the dark. There was pain in every element of his flesh. His organs swam within him like lethargic eels. His eyeballs were expanding their size to compete with his brain in the categories of ponderability and sphericity. Sudor crawled across his skin leaving itself behind in chilly traces which he had not the strength nor the will to wipe away. A woman visited him in his dream. She told him of the galactic column. Bellesgrant wept when he heard. The woman told him, *That column will never move.*

Zerxaquarius burned his garden to ashes, but this did not satisfy him, so he burned down his mansion as well. Still, Zerxaquarius perceived within himself the quenchless agony of time, and that was burning madly, so he went in search of cities to burn.

Bellesgrant descended through the levels. There was no bottom here, and there were always deeper levels. Bellesgrant devoted all his attention to the procedure by which his legs conveyed him from level to level. The levels were evenly spaced, and each appeared exactly similar to the others. There was no way to know how many levels he had descended, for he did not count them.

The world was depopulated. There were only two men left, and they were on opposite sides of the globe. He bellowed their names, but neither heard him. He beat his own head with a planchette he found in one of the deserted towns. He screamed, and screamed, and screamed: until his voice failed. At this point, he went into a deli and made a sandwich. He began to appreciate the silence.

Memoir of a Mouth

Chapter 1: Why I Weep

My corruption began in a bead of truth I found cradled in the crack between two slabs. The bead was of the color red. The bead shared its shape with the sphere. The bead was smooth as the glass of an old man's eye. I called the bead "Beauty" after her whom I have always sought. I believed the bead would lead me to her. I therefore gave myself into its leading.

I shed my morality then. I sank my teeth in flesh. I washed my face with blood. I attended the symphony of screams and congratulated its conductor, admiring his work while plotting his murder.

I entered Hell on my knees. I prayed, saying, "You dropped the bead, O Lord, and I picked it up because I was the innocent boy you made me. And I've been made corrupted, I've gone mad with what you left me to find—because I am the foolish boy you made me. I am now mad, and evil, and emptied of all joy.

"I pray thee, Lord, shall I leave the bead here, in the keeping of demons, shall I dispossess myself of Beauty—then please you to return me to what I was before my corruption began."

I dropped the bead into Hell's gully. I reentered this world, and in answer to my prayer, I am still corrupted.

Only, now, for my pains, I am without the bead.

Shall Beauty stand before me, I will not know her. And you wonder why I weep!

Chapter 2: Birth

My father told me, "Your body's flesh is the flame of your spirit's longing. Fire's way is to travel until it meets water. Therefore must you travel till you meet your destiny of water: she will be a beautiful one!"

My mother told me, "Your body's flesh is the dew of your spirit's discontent. Dew's way is to lie still upon the leaves until the sun's rising. Therefore must you lie still till you meet your destiny of morning: she will be a beautiful one!"

And I've spent my time in the world striving toward both flame and dew. Though my parents have gone to their graves, yet their advice has lived within me and guided the actions of my will.

I've traveled everywhere, and everywhere I've lain still.

And soon, perhaps, I'll go mad.

Or, perhaps, I'll set the seas to burning.

All the same, she'll not be beautiful. I've traveled for longing and lain still for discontent; destiny has given me only greater longing and further discontent.

She'll not be beautiful, no: her face will be a skull.

Mad, perhaps, I'll set the seas to burning.

Chapter 3: Love

I was in the city then. A girl's beauty enthralled me. There was a diamond in the center of her. Should it ever be uncovered to our vision, we'd all burn endlessly in its shining. I concluded, "At all costs, my mission shall be to uncover the diamond. It shall be my mission to reveal the diamond into my own hand."

I pursued her till she feared me. I pursued her till she set her brothers against me. They could not defend her from the likes of me, who commanded fires with my fingers and shook the earth under the laughter of my feet.

I pursued her till the world went quiet with its watching. The planet became still. The sky became red. The weather receded into space. The millions of the earth ceded liveliness to disease. And I pursued her till she went mad and knew not even herself, much less reason to fear me.

I peeled her to the bone, and revealed utterly to my eye the diamond in the center of her. My eye burned and wept its own flesh till there was only the empty socket of my skull to remember it.

Blinded, I traveled from the city to this countryside of darkness. Here, I keep the diamond always in my hand. I cannot see the diamond, but holding it, I am reminded of the beauty I have lusted after all my life.

Chapter 4: Death

I sat with the roots; their tree shaded me. The grasses said, "Take thee from sitting.

"Take thee to singing!

"Be no more these jumbled bones.

"Become the world's sweetest tones!"

O, who could obey the injunction? And worse, who could not? I begged advice of the roots; as always, they stayed silent. The grasses spoke no more. As alone as I was before, I was now. Everything around me was the same.

The sky was red, red as the tears weeping from my eyes. Yes, that was me writhing in the roots; I, myself, could hardly believe it. It began to rain. I became muddy. My movements ceased awhile, but soon—acclimated to the new, unclean condition of its flesh—my body commenced once more to writhing, yet more vigorously and more defiantly of the grasses, which observed without passion.

I battered at the roots; I stripped them bare; I bit them with my teeth; I tore them with my fingernails.

I battered at my own body. I strove against my bones. I scooped of my flesh as of water from a well.

The sky was red, red as my body weeping from my wounds. Yes, that was me exhausted in the roots. That was me, still, shaded by the tree. And the grasses said, "You've done enough!

"You're much too rough.

"But lay thee there!

"We just don't care."

O, and the ecstasy!

The rain began again, torrented over me. The grasses bowed, bent, and finally broke beneath the onslaught of too many waters. They washed away, and the peaceful night came on. More alone than I was before, I was now.

Everything around me was beautiful.

Afterword

Intimations of a Poetics
of the Infinite

On the Progress of a Molecule Across Eternity

How long shall you maintain that smile? How definitive an answer is sought? The moment of wondering itself will finish it off.

You will be left with the feeling that everything passed by while you were occupied discerning visions from shadows on an irrelevant compass point, and of course, the truth is that you yourself passed by while everything—inert—observed your progress minutely and smiled in the inscrutable manner of inanimate objects.

But you fool no one: you have been aware of your cynical nonchalance all this while, quite knowingly out of the loop, your calculated innocence obvious to every insentient being that cast a beam on you.

A merriment cascades through your sensitive body, and equally through the infested milk in which you swim, concentric waves, radiant from your spine's base, obliterating the vagabond malcontents with a neverending enfilade of chortles and smirks, crowds of fey bacteria swarming to their communal death, lactic and lachrymose.

That is very much in line with reality, isn't it? The argument never really is with Other, always with yourself. You are your own Other. That's the tragedy. Failure to perceive one's own duality.

What a lie that is.

Truly, the tragedy is too quick perception of one's own duality.

Eagerness!

Not to mention the imperative to blame genuine Others for disruptions caused by the imposter you made with your own hands out of *papier maché* so many years ago in a classroom that smelled of purple and glue. Meanwhile, the teacher snuck away to mimeograph the hymnal she transferred to her purse one idle Sunday morning. (And she thought I wasn't looking!)

Redemption incites the recrimination of Desire: "How could you dispose of me so cruelly? I thought you loved me!"

Yet move to satisfy her, and you will be met with wailing: "You haven't done enough! You never even try!"

In either case, better to burn than to meet her eye.

A Little Light Rain

One might spend a day tabulating the synaptic randomness of a minute. Mostly it jumps over you, unheeded, its ineluctable weirdness cloaked in height. But sometimes, the car bounces, the body raises, the attention finds itself mired in details. Don't worry, gravity soon works upon you, and the storm is left to rampage in the clouds, rarely dropping thunderbolts to electrify your habitat.

You will find yourself deep in the past, flying above the ground you walked then, seeing what you missed, refashioning what you failed to ignore. A diamond ring made blue and pink in the light of future color. A lover with the dog in her lap and the sun in her eyes. A doubled rainbow clenching the mountain caps in its vise.

Be not afraid of the rain. True, it will bring the mud, but it will also clean the car.

Be grateful to the tide. Be grateful to History. The wind decides. The moon needs only to purse her lips to elicit your moaning. Be grateful to the kiss. Run unfettered by your memory of the flood's rising bliss, and you will be rewarded with the submerged streetlamp's flickering nocturnal simulacrum of sexual ecstasy.

Things end as they do, and we always see it coming. Yet there is no greater surprise.

First Comes Revelry, Then Comes Reveille

There is a summit in the east the sun must climb each morning. Some days the sun is weak from the exertion; other days the sun's energy is rampant on the trees.

When you hear the hawk cry, it is time to cower in your house, for that is the only sound that might pierce the jelly of the sun. Who knows what will fall from heaven before the day is done? *Feign horror*, though I know you're not afraid! Cower in the cellar among the dangling willow roots. The act is paramount over the impulse.

When the safe bath of moonlight has risen gently lapping at the lip of your tub tonight, take care not to lean back so far that your face is covered. The saturation of the lungs by soft light has been known to cause ascension into unsavory cosmic spheres. . . . Some have not returned. Those that have come back will not speak, but their eyes remain perpetually open in a gaze that sees everything but recognizes nothing. It is an acknowledged phenomenon, even though the scientific community rejects the notion in its journals. (To truly know the mind of the scientist, read his blog, not his peer-reviewed piffle.)

An insect is needed in the witching hour. It will light the way to the next hill. Once you've mounted to the top, your light will blind them all. The fools won't see you, but you should force them to their knees. That, after all, is the purpose of godhood. Don't fail them—they'll despise you more for your squeamishness than your malice.

The beauty of rage is its grace. Its fire destroys everything equally under the sun. Would you have it any other way, Milady?

Everything We Need to Know

There are so many like us. . . . Have we spent an hour on the train only to realize we never got on—that was someone else? Have we entertained a friend at home only to realize that he was a stranger? Have we spoken in stentorian manly voices only to look down and notice the milky trails from our teats?

And waking from the dream to be depluralized. Oh, the collective memory that brings me my childhood. The anonymous crowd that I was when I threw Joey into the rafters of the gym. The group of sinners kicking that boy in the ribs. So many souls rushing to fill the spaces I occupy.

And if you feel it so deeply, from one cavern's end to the other, if it is so privately cherished, then why do you broadcast it to such a distant coordinate? There may be a mile of earth between you and open air, and yet the citizens of Pleiades know every contour of your mind, have studied your modalities with a compulsive curiosity that cannot be shaken clear of minds so otherwise noble. Are you some virus sent to plague them, some unshakable meme that shall outlast their civilization, unearthed and resuscitated by future interstellar archaeologists?

The frisson of recognition occurs readily across the gaps of generations, so that DNA is our totem, genes are time travelers; words unravel us briefly, but we are soon woven back into the burlap spirit. . . .

Look to Toltecs and Tolstoy. Everything one needs to know is there.